What do
you want to
do for fun,
Murphy?

Let's go on the train to visit our friends!

Hello Sammy the Seal from Squamish—jump on board.

Fred the Black Bear is waiting for us in Kamloops.

and Charlie the Goat will be at the station in Revelstoke.

All aboard Fred!

Off to The North to visit my friend
Carol the Caribou in Prince George.

Here comes Jerry the Duck and Spinner
the Hummingbird from Williams Lake.

Now let's go to Kelowna to visit Dave the Seagull and Slick the Otter. Maybe we will see Ogopogo!

Say Hello to Mama Grizzly and her 3 new cubs, Biggsy, Normy and Rudy from Salmon Arm.

Thanks for coming on our Fun Train Ride!

© Copyright 2009 Peter Scarth.

All rights reserved. No part of this publication may be reproduced, stored in a retrieval system, or transmitted, in any form or by any means, electronic, mechanical, photocopying, recording, or otherwise, without the written prior permission of the author.

Illustrations by: Cathy Angus-Healey
Edited by: Eleanor Scarth

Note for Librarians: A cataloguing record for this book is available from Library and Archives Canada at www.collectionscanada.ca/amicus/index-e.html

Printed in Victoria, BC, Canada.

ISBN: 978-1-4251-8630-2

*We at Trafford believe that it is the responsibility of us all, as both individuals and corporations, to make choices that are environmentally and socially sound. You, in turn, are supporting this responsible conduct each time you purchase a Trafford book, or make use of our publishing services. To find out how you are helping, please visit www.trafford.com/responsiblepublishing.html*

*Our mission is to efficiently provide the world's finest, most comprehensive book publishing service, enabling every author to experience success. To find out how to publish your book, your way, and have it available worldwide, visit us online at www.trafford.com/10510*

www.trafford.com

**North America & international**
toll-free: 1 888 232 4444 (USA & Canada)
phone: 250 383 6864 ♦ fax: 250 383 6804
email: info@trafford.com

**The United Kingdom & Europe**
phone: +44 (0)1865 487 395 ♦ local rate: 0845 230 9601
facsimile: +44 (0)1865 481 507 ♦ email: info.uk@trafford.com

10 9 8 7 6 5 4 3 2